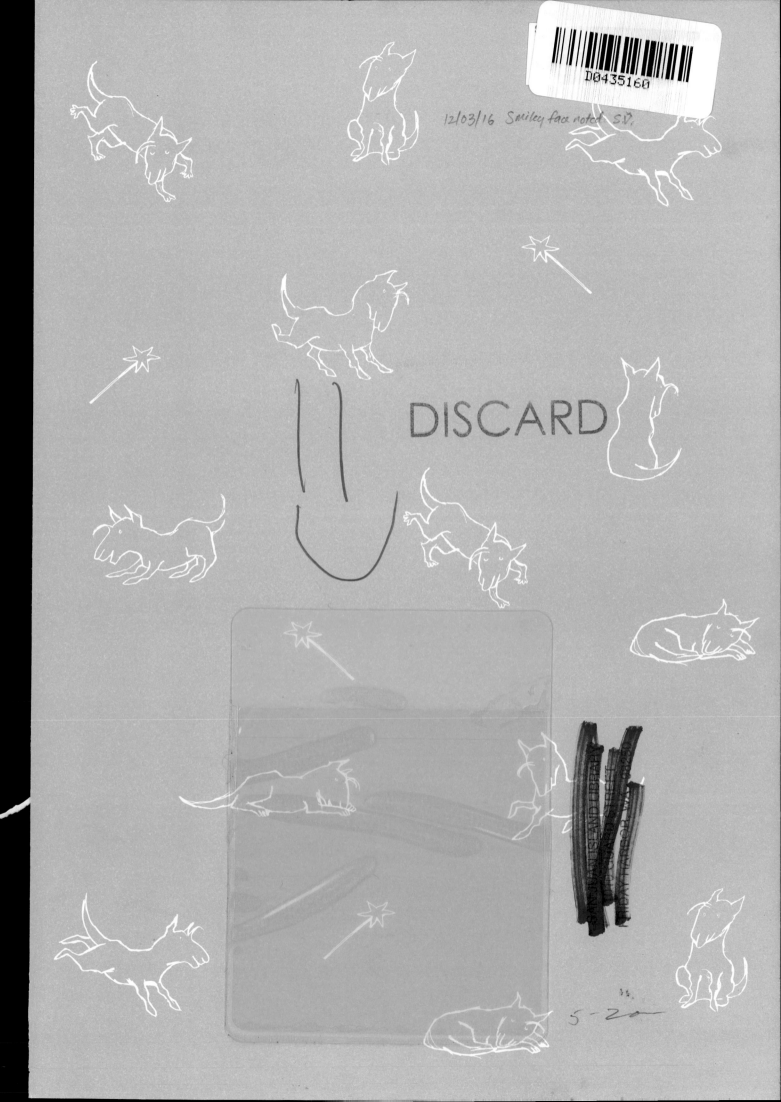

I Wished for a Unicorn

Written by
Robert Heidbreder

Illustrated by
Kady MacDonald Denton

Kids Can Press

I wished for a unicorn.
I wished so hard
That I found a unicorn
In my backyard.

I was sitting alone
By our old oak tree
When I saw a unicorn
Looking at me.

He was kind of scruffy
And he'd lost his horn.
But I knew at once
He was a unicorn.

He didn't have a mane.
His tail wagged around.
He chomped on a bone
Dug up from the ground.

His ears flopped about
In a happy way.
His tongue hung out
'Cause he wanted to play.

He didn't neigh softly,
As unicorns do.
He barked and he howled
And he yowled — aaaaOOOOOO!

But he was a unicorn
Without any doubt.
He pawed and he pranced
And he galloped about.

Then he led me away
To a magical wood,
As only a real live
Unicorn could.

We crept and we crawled
Under darkening skies,

Past creatures that frowned,
'Round trees that had eyes.

We spotted a castle
That rose in the air.
We rushed to its moat —
What danger lurked there?

'Cross the water we flew
With a leap and a bound

And landed — KERPLOP! —
On the castle's hard ground.

We spied magic wands
Near a secret door

And stormed the castle
With a thunderous roar!

We zapped a fierce dragon

And stopped it from flying.

We shrunk an evil wizard —

He ran away crying!

We found a treasure map,
All crumpled and old.

So we fled from the castle
To find buried gold.

We dug a hundred holes
And we dug them deep,

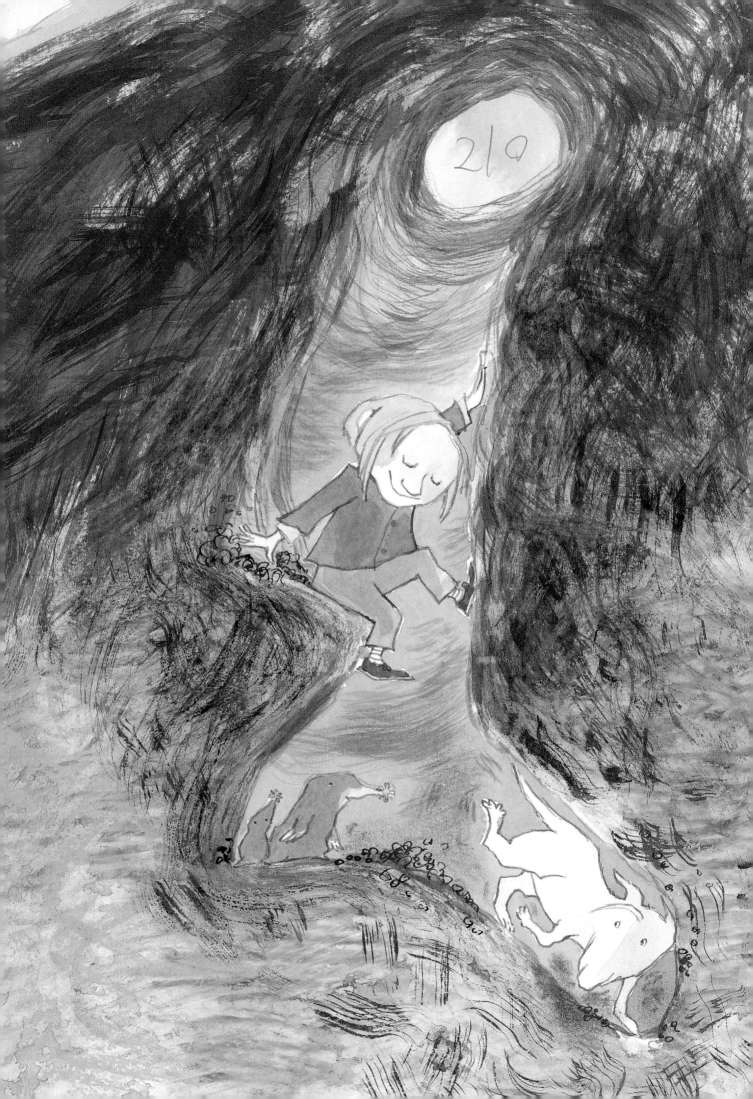

Till we both grew tired

And fell fast asleep.

But when I woke up
    With a stretch and a yawn,
There was only my dog
    Asleep on the lawn.

I think that tomorrow
    When I go out to play,
I'll wish once again
    For a unicorn day.

I'll wish for a unicorn
Under my tree,
And I bet that I'll find
A unicorn for me!

To Susie, my sister and childhood playmate — R.H.

For Ricky — K.M.D.

Kids Can Press acknowledges the support of the Ontario Arts Council, the Canada Council for the Arts and the Government of Canada, through the BPIDP, for our publishing activity. Canada

Published in Canada by
Kids Can Press Ltd.
29 Birch Avenue
Toronto, ON M4V 1E2

Published in the U.S. by
Kids Can Press Ltd.
4500 Witmer Industrial Estates
Niagara Falls, N.Y. 14305-1386

The artwork in this book was rendered in gouache.
Text is set in Gill Sans.

Edited by Tara Walker
Designed by Kady MacDonald Denton
Printed and bound in Hong Kong by Book Art Inc., Toronto

CM 00 0 9 8 7 6 5 4 3 2 1

Canadian Cataloguing in Publication Data

Heidbreder, Robert
    I wished for a unicorn

ISBN 1-55074-543-3

I. Denton, Kady MacDonald. II. Title.

PS8565.E4219 2000   jC813'.54   C99-932135-8
PZ7.H44Iw 2000

Kids Can Press is a Nelvana company